A VERY CAMPBELL CHRISTMAS

WENDY SMITH

Edited by
CREATING INK

Cover Design by
BOOKISH GRAPHICS

This book is written in New Zealand English, and as such contains phrasing and kiwi colloquialisms.

�֍ Created with Vellum

ONE

DREW

DRIVING to Copper Creek on Christmas Eve is both idiotic and unavoidable.

The traffic will be the pits, but at the same time, it also marks the start of our Christmas holidays, which we're spending with family.

Dad offered to look after the kids for the week of New Year because I plan to whisk my wife away for a romantic break. So, it's not really all that bad.

But even the act of getting out of our driveway seems to be difficult.

"Come on, you guys. Get in the car."

"Daaaaad, we just want to finish this game," Amelia pleads.

I sigh. "You were given plenty of warning. Turn that Xbox off and move your butt."

"But, Dad." Logan joins her, and I look at the ceiling.

"Double trouble, alright," I mutter under my breath.

"Don't grumble. You love it." Hayley grins.

I shift my gaze to her. Her eyes are so full of love, and she never fails to take my breath away when she looks at me like that.

"You know it. But we do have to get going. It's such a long drive."

She rubs my back. "I know, but we've got two whole weeks of holiday, and one of those is just you and me."

I wink at her. "Now you're talking."

Hayley laughs. "Come on, guys. Let's get in the car. Dad's keen to get going."

"Mum? Please?" Amelia asks.

We keep them on their toes taking turns playing good cop, bad cop. I used to think I wanted a ton of kids, but three turned out to be the right number. I'm not sure I could cope with more.

"No. Turn that off, or I will." She gives them a stern look.

"But ..."

Hayley's raised eyebrow stops Amelia in her tracks. Fuck, I love my wife. If we didn't have to get on the road, I'd leave the kids to play on the damn Xbox and lock ourselves in our bedroom for a while.

"Alex is already waiting in the car. She's my favourite today," I throw over my shoulder as I walk toward the front door.

"Drew. Oh my God." Hayley gawks at me then covers her amused face with her hand. "You can't say that."

"Why not? It's true. I don't think we can stop for ice cream on the way either. We're not going to have time." I step out into the sunshine and smile as our twins go flying past me to get to the car.

"You know that's not going to work forever," Hayley says, walking up behind me.

I slide my arm around her waist. "I know, but I'll use it until it doesn't."

"You're such a dick."

"I know that. You know that. But the kids don't know. Let them work it out for themselves."

She leans her head against mine. "Between you and me, I think they already know."

THE FIRST HOUR of the journey flies by.

There's silence in the back seat, which is pretty unusual considering there's normally an argument by now. It concerns me as much as I enjoy the peace.

"Are we stopping for ice cream?" I ask.

"Yes."

I sigh with content. It's our Campbell family tradition to stop at a small dairy by the side of the road for ice cream.

"I bet you guys are looking forward to playing in the playground for a while."

From the rear-view mirror, I see Alexandra roll her eyes.

I think she'll be the one who follows in my footsteps. She's the quiet, studious one, reading books way beyond her ten years and, at this stage, wants to be a doctor. Logan and Amelia are competitive in every way possible, and I have no idea what they'll end up being.

The love I have for all of them is fierce, even if they all misbehave from time to time.

"Dad, why couldn't we take the Xbox to Poppa's?" Logan asks.

"Doesn't Max have one that lives there?"

"It's so old," he says.

"Oh well, it'll be a retro couple of weeks, then."

"It's so boring in Copper Creek," Amelia says.

"We can go to the beach every day." Alex pipes up, and I don't miss Amelia mimicking her.

"Leave your sister alone. I grew up there. It's only as boring as you want it to be. There's plenty to do."

I shoot a glance at Hayley. She's biting her lip in amusement. Copper Creek's not just special to me because I spent a chunk of my life there. It's special because that's where I met her.

That turned out to be the best day of my life, and one I've never regretted.

She gave me our beautiful family and put her life at risk doing it.

I love this woman to the moon and back. Hayley's not just my wife, she's my best friend. Who also happens to double as my business partner. It took a while to coax her out of her semi-retirement after we had the kids, but she now works with me in my private obstetrics practice.

She worried that spending too much time together would be a bad thing, but, instead, it's been the opportunity to find those quiet moments with each other without three pre-teens around.

It's working for us.

"It's nearly time to stop for ice cream. Have you worked out what you want?" she asks.

"Boysenberry ripple," Alex says.

"Vanilla," the twins chorus. It brings a smile to my lips. They fight like cat and dog, but still share the same taste in nearly everything.

"Same thing as every other year," Hayley says.

I reach for her hand and drag it to my lips before I settle it on the gearstick, under mine. She smiles, looking back out the window.

The drive isn't too bad. It's a beautiful summer's day, and the warm breeze that flows through the car relaxes me as the kilometres slip by.

I pull into a park outside our usual dairy stop. It's not any particular brand, but their servings are generous, especially for the kids, and the cheapest I've seen anywhere. And it's about the halfway point of our trip, so breaks it up nicely.

Leading my family into the store, the bell above the door chimes as we walk through. Numerous freezers span the room, each lit up with tubs of ice cream in various colours and flavours, a rainbow of whipped dairy goodness.

I take a deep breath, notes of vanilla, chocolate, and caramel so sweet I nearly get a toothache.

IT ALMOST SEEMS BORING to buy our usual flavours. Vanilla for the twins, boysenberry ripple for Alex, and orange with chocolate chips for Hayley and me.

"Let's go and sit in the park," I say.

Logan looks at me. "We're sitting in the car."

"What?"

"Can you unlock it please, Dad?"

All three of my children walk back to the car. You'd think they'd be sick of sitting on their butts, but, apparently, not. I huff as I press the key fob to unlock it.

"Are you okay?" Hayley touches my arm.

"No. When did our kids get so grown up?"

"It happens. Why don't we sit in the park?"

I cast another glance back at the car. "Good idea. I'll eat some ice cream with my favourite girl. At least you don't desert me."

She smiles. "Never."

I hand her my ice cream then walk over to the car, and Alex looks up in surprise when I open the driver's door.

"I'm just leaving you guys the keys in case you want to listen to some music. Mum and I are heading over to the park for a bit." I slide the key into the ignition and turn it until the radio comes on.

I close the door and make my way back to Hayley.

She holds out my cone, a sneaky glint in her eyes, but only relinquishes it after I've kissed her lips.

Taking her free hand in mine, we stroll the short distance to the empty park bench before taking a seat. I pull her into my side, and she snuggles against me.

I love our life, and our children, but I just feel like they're leaving us behind.

Is it possible to have empty nest syndrome while they still live with you?

"I miss them playing, too," she says, as if knowing that's

what I'm thinking. "But we have to get used to them growing up. They're not going to stop."

I laugh. "I know. I guess I just used to feel needed more than I am now."

Hayley sits up, her gaze meeting mine. "You'll always be needed. Maybe it won't seem like it, but they'll never not need you." She licks her lips. "And then there are my needs."

Grinning, I press my forehead to hers. "Oh, I hope I always meet those needs."

"You've never let me down, yet."

"Glad to hear it." I lean back.

Haley snuggles back in. "I've never had any regrets with you. Not a single minute."

"I can think of a few minutes you might have regretted."

She laughs. "Fine. Since we got married. Are you happy?"

A melted drop forms at the top of her cone, so I scoop it up before it lands on her shirt then suck it off my finger.

"I'm always happy when I'm with you, princess."

As much as I mourn my children growing up, I love them being independent enough for Hayley and me to be able to share moments together.

The seat beside me sinks as if a ton of weight just hit it, so I turn to see not one but all three of our children sitting beside us.

Amelia's closest, and she smiles as I slip my free arm around her shoulders. She snuggles into my other side.

"We locked the car, Dad. Here are the keys." Logan places them on my lap.

"Dad, can we stay here a little longer?" Alex asks from next to Amelia.

"Sure we can."

"I want to play on the playground."

I stare over Amelia's head at her. "Really? I thought you were too old for that."

"I'm not sure you're ever too old," Hayley says.

"Go on. We can wait here for a bit."

I take a deep breath as the three of them launch off the bench, running toward the swings and slides, their laughter filling the air around us.

Hayley pulls back and looks at me. "Happy?"

"Very."

AN HOUR LATER, we're back on the road.

The silence that filled the first part of our journey is gone as the three of them talk about movies, TV shows, and YouTube videos they've watched.

This is what I've missed.

When we reach Dad's place, the doors of the car are thrown open, and they spill out onto the lawn and run toward the house to see their grandfather.

Hayley and I are left in their dust.

"We survived the road trip," Hayley says as I round the car.

I slip my arm around her waist. "Think we can sneak off now instead of waiting a week?"

She pushes me back. "I'm not sure we can get away with that."

"Shame." I bury my nose in the back of her neck. "I guess we should go in and see Dad."

She leans her head back. "We should. But maybe we could just stay like this for a moment."

"I love you." I breathe in the vanilla scent of her skin.

"I love you too." She lets out a contented sigh. "I might even love you after the kids have grown up and moved out."

"They're never moving out. I won't let them."

Hayley laughs and turns to face me. "I don't think you get a say in it."

"I will if I lock them in their rooms forever."

She reaches up, cupping my cheek. "There's still a lot of time left before they leave home. I'm sure we can find ways of keeping occupied."

I raise my eyebrows. "I like the way you think, princess."

She bites her bottom lip. "Have I ever told you just how much I love you calling me that?"

"I don't think so. Do you know why I call you that?"

"No."

"I just always wanted to be your prince."

Her expression softens and her eyes fill with longing. "Did you just make that up?"

"Maybe, but does it matter?"

My beautiful wife gives me a lingering kiss and sighs. "I like it. Keep that up and I might even stay married to you."

"That's my girl."

TWO

JAMES

"YOU GUYS ALL GOOD FOR TOMORROW?" Adam closes the bonnet of the car he's been working on and looks at me.

I nod. "We'll be there around ten."

He walks across the workshop and grips my shoulder. "Merry Christmas, little brother."

"Same to you."

As he walks away, I pull my phone out of my pocket.

Mia: *Are you finishing work soon? We're down at the cove.*

That makes me grin. It doesn't take a genius to work out MacKenzie talked her mother into taking her to the beach. She's always been a real water baby.

Me: *Just cleaning up and I'll be on my way. Fish and chips for dinner? I'll grab some and bring them down.*

Mia: *Sweet talker. Sounds good to me.*

I walk out the back to my work locker and strip off my

overalls before washing off any grease and pulling my jeans on. Never in a million years did I think I'd end up working with Adam and Max.

Mia writes textbooks now. You can take the woman out of the university, but apparently you can't take the university out of the woman. She asks me sometimes if I have any regrets studying all that time before abandoning any career in biotech to become a mechanic.

All this time, and I've never had any regrets. Not about my career, and never about spending the years at university. Those years gave me her.

Leaving Adam to finish locking up, I head out to my Kia Sorento and start up the car. The fish and chip shop is not far down the road, but I'll head straight out to the cove once I've got the food.

After pulling up outside, I get out and lock the car, grinning as I spot Owen through the large glass window with numerous crustaceans painted on it.

He's at the back of the queue and buried in his phone, and looks up, blankly, as I tap him on the shoulder.

"Hey." He smiles. "Fish and chips for dinner?"

I nod. "Mia and MacKenzie are at the cove. I'm heading down there now." I pull my wallet out of my pocket as we move along the queue. "Why don't you bring the family down and we could have dinner together?"

Owen shakes his head. "No can do. We're having a quick dinner, and then Ava's got some party she's going to."

I chuckle. "I'm surprised you're letting her out of the house."

"It's not that I want to ..." He sighs. "Don't let MacKenzie grow up. All of a sudden she'll be sixteen and wanting to hang out with boys."

"I'll take that under advisement." I smile to myself.

"The thought of it is giving me grey hair. Seriously."

I bite down a laugh. "Owen, that's just old age."

He narrows his gaze. "That's enough of that."

"I'm sorry, but it's true." I nudge his elbow. "Your turn."

"Payback's going to be a bitch, little bro." He turns away and it's all I can do not to laugh as he steps up to the counter to make his order.

I pull my card out of my wallet, ready to place my order, and step up as Owen walks away.

"Hey, Brit. Could I please order the twenty-dollar bundle? With the hot dog instead of the crab sticks."

She taps it into the computer.

"That's forty-five dollars."

I stare at her. "Sorry?"

"You're paying for Owen's too, aren't you? That's what he told me."

I turn my head to look at my brother, who's now leaning against the glass window. He lifts his chin, and I roll my eyes before turning back. "Fine. Whatever. I'll pay for his too."

Waving my card over the EFTPOS machine, I wait for the receipt before walking over to where he's standing.

He cocks his head. "Think of it as your Christmas present to me."

I laugh. "Well played. I guess I'll just eat that big box of chocolates Mia bought you."

"Oh no, they're all mine. Your lady has good taste in presents."

Shaking my head, I sigh. "I'll find a way to get you back."

"I'm sure you will."

While we wait, I pull out my phone and scroll my social media. It's the easiest way to stay in touch with people I never see since we moved to Copper Creek.

Cody is onto what seems like his fifteenth girlfriend of the year, and Ashley's post makes me smile. She went back to Auckland to finish studying, met and fell in love with a really good guy, and is now heavily pregnant with their second child.

I used to regret what happened between her and me, but following Ashley to Auckland in the first place was what led me to Mia. We both got the happy endings we were supposed to.

Owen nudges my arm. "Dinner's ready."

I look up to see Brit smiling our way and holding two parcels.

We walk up together and collect them before making our way out the door.

"See you tomorrow," Owen calls as he walks away.

I just shake my head as I climb into the car, dropping the food bundle onto the seat next to me.

It's not a long drive out to the beach, and I drop the window and take a breath of that warm sweet air that flows through the car.

The garage is now closed for Christmas and New Year, except for emergencies. And in a town like Copper Creek, thankfully that doesn't happen too often.

Pulling into the car park, I grab the food, climb out of the car, and walk toward the beach. Earlier today, there would have been a ton of people here with school finishing a few days ago, but it's fairly quiet this time of day. Most would have gone home to prepare for Christmas tomorrow.

Mia has a blanket spread out on the sand, and she's sitting facing the water, taking in the rays with a book in her hands.

"Hey, beautiful."

She turns her head to look at me. In her fifties, my wife is as beautiful as she's ever been. She's so self-conscious about the tinge of grey in her hair, but I'm more in love with her every day. Mia's my foundation.

"Hey, yourself. You bought dinner?"

I hold up the paper package. "I did. Most expensive fish and chips ever."

Her brows knit. "Why?"

"Somehow I ended up paying for Owen's as well. Payback is gonna be a bitch."

She laughs as I take a seat next to her.

"Good day?" I ask.

Mia nods. "Just enjoying the sun. It's so peaceful out here."

I smile. "Where's MacKenzie?"

Mia points toward the water. "Right over there."

My girl stands by the water's edge.

"Is she okay?"

"As okay as you get when you're a pre-teen with hormones starting to rage through your system?"

I chuckle. "That good, huh?"

"She's really moody. I think she's been looking forward to seeing her dad."

"I've been looking forward to seeing my girls. And now

the garage is shut up for the holidays, I get to spend the next three weeks with you two."

She drops her book on the blanket and leans back with her hands behind her. "It feels like it's taken forever to get to today."

"At least you don't have to worry about Christmas dinner tomorrow." I lean over and kiss my wife on the lips. "I asked Lily again if she wanted us to bring something, but you know what she's like."

Mia nods. "Oh, I know. But I've got a trifle in the fridge to take whether she likes it or not. I know you'll eat it if there's too much food."

I kiss her again. "Speaking of food ... We should eat. I'll go get the munchkin."

"Good luck. Maybe she'll not be so cranky with you."

Pushing myself to my feet, I shrug. "I'll have a word with her. Be back in a minute."

MacKenzie stands at the water's edge, kicking her toes in the water, and even at a distance she looks deep in thought. That's my kid. She'll probably end up being an academic like her mother.

"Hey, kiddo."

MacKenzie looks up. Her smile is infectious. It always is. Her dark hair and blue eyes make her a mini Mia. One day she'll break a lot of hearts.

"Dad, how did you know we were here?"

"Your mum sent me a text. I brought dinner. What have you been doing?"

She digs her toes into the sand, twisting her foot. "Mum got sick of hanging around the house, so we came down here."

"Are you feeling okay?"

I open my arms to her, and she falls into them. "I'm just glad you're home."

"Me too. It's Christmas tomorrow, and we get to spend it with your cousins. You must be looking forward to that. Amelia, Logan, and Alex will be there. I know how much you like spending time with them."

She sniffs. "I do."

"What's wrong?"

She looks up at me with her mother's eyes. This child who was never meant to be is our miracle. I don't think she'll ever know just how much Mia and I love her.

"Are you my dad?"

I raise my hand and brush her dark hair from her face. "You know I am. Why are you asking?"

She sighs. "Ben and I were googling stuff, and I googled Mum. There was all this stuff about her at the university, and she had a different name. It said she was married."

My insides turn to liquid. No wonder she's moody if she's read something and interpreted it that way. "No, honey. She was married to someone before she met me. But they weren't together when we fell in love." I kiss her on the forehead. "And then I whisked her away to live here so we could be close to family, and then we had you."

Her eyes widen. "Oh."

"You could have asked Mum about it."

Her bottom lip quivers. "I thought she might get angry with me."

"Your mother angry with you? When has *that* ever happened?"

MacKenzie laughs. "Never."

"She loves you, and she deserves better than you getting moody about something like that without asking her about it."

"Sorry, Dad."

"Go and give her a hug. She loves you so much."

Mia stands as we approach. I'm sure she's been watching us from the beach, and her whole face lights up as MacKenzie throws her arms around her and buries her face in Mia's chest.

"Everything okay?" she mouths.

"Everything's fine." I mouth back. Tugging on MacKenzie's ponytail, I plant a kiss on the top of her head. "How about we eat before the food gets cold."

IT'S JUST after seven when we get home. I unlock the door and stand back to let Mia through first before stepping into the living room.

"Dad, get out of the way. I need the bathroom." MacKenzie shoves me, and I step sideways to let her through.

Mia drops her bag on the floor beside the couch and turns toward me.

"What was all that about at the beach? That looked like a pretty intense conversation you were having with MacKenzie."

I cross the room and look into her eyes. "Nothing gets past you, does it?"

Mia's lips twitch. "Not often. She seemed much better after she spoke to you."

I pull my wife into my arms and give her a gentle kiss on the lips. "She looked you up on the internet and got a bit confused when she found you had a last name she didn't know about."

Mia's mouth falls open. "It's been Campbell for ten years now. That must have been confusing for her."

I nod. "It was. She asked me if I was really her father."

Mia blinks rapidly, dropping her gaze from mine. "I wish she'd just asked me. No wonder she was so moody."

"It's sorted now." I scan her expression. "It just left her a little unsettled."

"She did seem to switch moods after Ben was over here earlier."

I nod. "Those two are close. I might have a word with Adam, too, in case his son thinks I'm not MacKenzie's dad."

"He's like a brother to her." Mia sighs. "I'll always wonder if she would have been happier with a sibling." Her eyes fill with tears. "I wish I'd met you earlier. I wish we'd had time ..."

I pull my wife in close and hug her tight. "What we have is perfect. Babe, we didn't even expect to get MacKenzie. Every day, the two of you make me happy. I have no regrets, and neither should you."

"But ..."

"Besides. If we'd met too much earlier, it would have been teenage me, and that boy was such a mess."

Her lips spread into a wide smile. "You were never a mess."

"Want a bet? There was a time I didn't even want to go to

uni because Mum was sick, and I thought my place was here. Adam slapped some sense into me."

"Then it's Adam I owe a great debt to."

"I'm the one who owes him." I gaze into her beautiful blue eyes and shake my head. "Merry Christmas, Mia." I wipe her tears away with my thumb and kiss her softly. "I love you."

"Love you too."

The springs on the couch squeak, and we both turn to see MacKenzie bounce as she sits.

"Mum, did Dad tell you what happened?"

Mia nods, pulls away from me, and walks over to our daughter. She sits beside her and tugs her into her arms. "He did. It hurts you didn't ask me about it. We've got nothing to hide from you, MacKenzie."

MacKenzie buries her face in her mother's chest. "I'm sorry."

"You don't need to apologise. You saw something you didn't understand, and it must have worried you." Mia rubs MacKenzie's back. "But I want you to know just how much your dad and I love you." Mia looks over at me. "I met your dad at a really bad time in my life, and he made everything better. And then we made you. You were the icing on the cake. I'll never love anyone more than I love you and your father."

I sit on the other side of MacKenzie. "I feel the same way about you two."

"How about we get dad to make his famous hot chocolate, and we'll put on our pyjamas and watch TV. There's bound to be a Christmas movie on, and you know how much he loves them." Mia smirks before burying her face in MacKenzie's hair.

MacKenzie shakes with laughter, raising her head to look at me. "Dad hates them."

"I take it all back. You two were sent to torture me." I laugh. "Three hot chocolates coming up. Who's going to be back to the couch first to drink them?"

MacKenzie snaps her head in my direction. "Me!"

"Better beat your mother because she's pretty quick."

She leaps up, running toward the stairs.

Mia smiles at me. "Think she's okay?"

I nod. "She'll be fine. Like you said, she's probably at an uncertain age enough as it is."

"What are we going to do when she's a full-blown teenager?"

"Send her to live with Owen. I'm sure he doesn't have enough on his hands with an actual teenager *and* a pre-teen."

She laughs. "You're still sore about him scamming you into paying for his dinner."

"Always." I reach for her hand. "I'm glad you're smiling."

Mia sighs. "It's not easy dealing with a daughter going through puberty when you're going through menopause."

I shuffle over and slide my arm around her shoulders. "I wonder if I can convince Owen to take her home tomorrow night. I'm sure she'd love a sleepover with Violet, and then you and me could have a night alone."

Mia's eyes shine with happiness. "Now you're talking."

"Mum! What are you doing? I beat you."

We turn to see MacKenzie standing in the doorway, her hands on her hips.

Mia puts her hands up in surrender. "Okay, okay. I'll be back in a minute."

As she stands, I swipe her backside. "Don't take too long."

"Hey!" Mia laughs.

"Dad, you're supposed to be making the hot chocolate. Hurry up."

I chuckle and push myself to my feet. "Okay, bossy bum. I'm on it."

As I walk into the kitchen to make my girls some drinks, it's hard not to feel like the luckiest man on the planet. I'm right where I need to be with two people I love more than anything else in the world.

And they love me right back.

THREE
COREY

"DAD."

Eli runs for me as soon as I step out of the truck. My boy hurls himself into my arms as he usually does, and I lean back against the door. "Oof. You're getting too big for that."

"Mum said so too."

My eyebrows rise. "I hope you haven't been giving your mother a hard time."

He shakes his head. "No. She's got her feet up and I made her a cup of tea."

Grinning, I ruffle his hair. "You're a good man."

"Are you home now? No more work?"

I nod. "Sure am. No work for a while. Not until after the baby's born."

His smile always hits me right in the chest. Eli's the one most like me with his height and facial features. Oscar and Isla have the same dainty features Constance has. I love them all something fierce, but I think Eli will be the one who follows in my footsteps.

The overwhelming need to see Con fills me, even though I only saw her hours before. All these years and she's my person. Always.

"Come on, Dad," Eli says.

I love the shit out of this kid. He's here, greeting me every day when I come home. That's if I'm not the one who picks him up from school. But school finished for the summer a week ago. With our newest baby due in a couple of weeks, our family's having an extended break, all together.

He zooms off ahead of me, and I just shake my head and follow toward our home.

Stepping inside the door, my heart feels full as I take in the sight of my very pregnant wife, her dark hair thrown up in a mess of coffee-coloured curls and her swollen feet up on an ottoman. I've never loved her more.

Her face lights up as she catches sight of me.

I kick off my boots, cross the room and lean over the back of the couch to kiss Constance, lingering on her lips. "How was your day?"

She leans back. "I could do with a sleep."

"Go and have one. I'll cook dinner." I walk around and take her by the hand.

Her eyes are heavy, and she has so little colour in her cheeks. The third trimester of pregnancy takes it out of her. After Isla, we'd decided not to have any more babies. But a combination of my procrastination over getting a vasectomy and Con's feeling that we weren't quite finished, won over.

This little one will be the last.

"I'll be fine."

"No. I'm home now, so go and take a nap. If you're still asleep when dinner's ready, I'll get the kids fed and to bed and join you."

She lets me help her up off the couch. "If you insist."

"I do, sweetness. You need as much rest as possible, and I know these three are a handful at times."

Constance wraps her arms around my waist and snuggles in tight. "They've been pretty good. Eli tries to help."

"It'll be easier when we're in the new house and have more room."

We cleared some land behind this place a while ago, and a new home for us has been my passion project, but with a bit of urgency behind it because we need more space. We built another room onto the house when Oscar was born, but when Isla came along, it became obvious we couldn't just keep adding on.

Our new home will be five bedrooms, which was prophetic given Constance's advanced stage of pregnancy. It has everything we love about the existing house, but we'll be able to spread out, and the current house will be moved to another section we bought, closer to town, with a view to turning it into a rental.

"Daddy." Isla throws herself at me while Oscar gives me the chin up from the hallway. I pull her up onto my hip.

"Hey, little sweetness. Let me help your mother for a minute and then you can tell me about your day."

She nods. "We did adding numbers today."

"Did you? You might have to teach it to your old dad."

Constance reaches up and runs her fingers through my

beard. "You stay here with her and I'll go and have a lie down. I'll probably get up before the kids go to bed because we have to get ready for Santa."

Isla's eyes grow wide. "Santa's here tomorrow, Daddy."

"I know he is. I bet he has some really cool shit for you."

"Corey." Constance laughs.

"Sorry. Stuff. I meant stuff." I press a kiss to her temple. "I'm just going to go and help your mother settle in for her nap, and I'll be back."

"I'll be fine. Stop fussing."

I let Isla drop to the ground. "I'm allowed to fuss. That's what husbands are for."

She pecks me on the lips. "That's what *my* husband does, apparently."

"Always. Come on."

I take her hand as we take the slow walk to the bedroom.

She screws up her face as she sits on the bed, her hand resting on her belly. Heat prickles through my body. I know that expression.

"Are you okay?"

Constance nods. "Braxton Hicks."

"Are you sure?" I've been with her through three pregnancies. The last one might have been a while ago, but I have a good memory.

"Just the odd twinge. There's no rhyme or reason to them. And, yes, I've called the midwife. I just need to get some sleep."

I frown. "Okay."

She squeezes my hand. "I'd tell you if there was anything wrong."

"Maybe I'll ask Drew to take a look at you in the morning."

Constance shakes her head. "It's Christmas, Corey. Let's just have a fun day with our children and I'll just sit on the couch and hold court."

I laugh. "Oh, you know you'll be the centre of attention." Turning, I head toward the door. "Oh, I forgot. I've got something for you. Give me a minute."

Leaving her on the bed, I head back out through the living room and tug on my boots at the door. Sitting in the glovebox of the truck are two Cadbury Flakes. They're Con's favourite and she asked me to get them this morning.

A bit of chocolate will bring a smile to her face.

Her eyebrow is cocked as I enter the room. "What are you up to?"

"Retrieving these from the truck." I hold up the chocolate bars and smile as her eyes widen.

"You remembered?"

"Of course I did. I'd be a pretty shitty husband if I forgot the one thing you asked me for today."

I sit down on the other side of the bed as she takes the chocolate from me and opens the wrapper on one of them. One bite, and she lets out a pleasured moan that goes straight to my cock.

"Watching you eat that is so fucking hot," I growl.

She chuckles and slides the bar into her mouth, taking another bite.

"Constance Campbell, I swear to God that if you keep this up, we can forget Christmas with the family because I'll be fucking you into that mattress."

Her tired smile tells me just how much she needs this rest.

"I love you," she says, her eyes full of affection.

"I love you too. Get some rest." Leaning down, I run my tongue around her lips, sweeping up the fragments of chocolate she missed. "Mm you do taste good."

"That's not the first time you've said that."

"Oh, you are in so much trouble later." I press another kiss to her lips and sit up. "But I have to focus on cooking dinner for the kids. I'll be back in here when I can."

She reaches to cup my face. "You're so good to me."

"That's the easiest thing in the world, sweetness."

With one more kiss, I get off the bed and head back into the kitchen. I love this time of day. The kids are all excited because I'm home, and I'm surrounded by love.

"Daddy, can we make chips?" Isla asks.

I ruffle her hair. "Sure thing. I'm sure there are some chicken pieces in the freezer. We can make some homemade nuggets. Does that go for all of you?"

Oscar beams, and Eli opens the freezer door. "I'll get the chicken."

"We're going to have a big lunch tomorrow at Uncle Adam's place, so we'll have something light for dinner. I'll make something for your mum when she wakes up."

Once everything's cooked and the kids are eating, I pop my head back into the bedroom and smile.

Con's fast asleep. She's lying diagonally across the bed and has her head on my pillow. And curled up beside her is Cassius. That damn dog knows better than to sleep on my bed, but I don't have the heart to move him.

He's far from the small Huntaway pup he used to be. He's old and arthritic, and he has barely left Con's side since I bought him for her all those years ago. I could always rely on him to keep her and the kids safe.

The thought of life without him makes me feel so empty. He opens one eye and looks at me as if to acknowledge I've caught him out. But I shake my head and turn to leave the room.

There's no point in telling him off. He's happy and he makes her happy.

After dinner, the kids wash up and get into their pyjamas.

Constance has already got a bottle of beer and a plate with a couple of Anzac biscuits ready to go for Santa. Isla places it on the coffee table like it's the most precious thing she's ever handled. I know Eli has long since stopped believing, and Oscar is pretty non-committal, but Isla's six and still clinging onto the idea that Santa's coming for a visit.

Neither of her brothers dissuade her, and I love them so much for it.

"Why don't we watch a movie and then go to bed?" I ask.

"Are you waiting for Santa too, Daddy?" Isla asks.

I plant a kiss on her forehead. "Of course. Doesn't everyone?"

Out of the corner of my eye, I spot Eli clapping his hand over his mouth and looking away.

I sit on the couch, Eli and Oscar on either side, with Isla on my lap. I'm not sure how this'll work with four children, but I can't wait to find out.

We're about half an hour into the movie when Isla, still cradled in my arms, snores softly.

I stand and carry her along the hallway to her bedroom. After two boys, Isla's my little princess, and her room reflects that. Whoever thought I'd have a bedroom in my house decorated almost entirely in pink?

I reach for the duvet and pull it back, gently lowering Isla into her bed. She snorts and rolls onto her side away from me, and I smile before planting a kiss on her temple.

"Night, night, little sweetness."

When I reach the door, I turn and take a look at her. She won't be my youngest for much longer, and I'm not much looking forward to her teenage years, but right now she's daddy's girl, and that fills my heart with more joy than I can handle.

OUR CHRISTMAS TRADITION is for Constance and me to put all the gifts under the tree, ready for the kids in the morning.

It's an evening we spend reminiscing over how we met, those early days of marriage and parenting, and usually ends with me giving my wife a special Christmas gift in our marital bed.

This year is different.

She's still fast asleep when I finally get to the bedroom. I gather the Christmas presents from the back of the wardrobe and carry them to the living room.

Constance will hate missing out on this part of the evening, but she's never been so pregnant at Christmas before, and she needs as much sleep as she can get.

One by one, I place the gifts under the tree.

At one point in my life, I never thought I'd have all this. Not just finding the right woman for me, but there's also the family we share. There was a time I thought I'd never be a father, and that I'd grow old alone on this mountain, still hung up on Lily.

One stormy night, Constance changed my life.

Here we are, celebrating another Christmas surrounded by our children. And the joy on their faces in the morning is worth all the hard work during the year.

Hell, ten years ago, I didn't think I'd ever have what would be considered a normal job, and then I was pretty old for an apprentice. But I did it, and now I have solid work all year round.

I wouldn't give up my life for anything.

After placing the gifts under the tree, I return to the bedroom and grab the gift I bought for Constance from the bottom of my bedside cabinet.

I saved all year to show her just how much she means to me. I know she'll hate how much I spent on her, but she's worth every cent.

The young woman who appeared in my backyard that night in the rain, turned out to be the love of my life.

I slip the present under the tree and return to the bedroom. She sleeps peacefully, well, as peacefully as she can when she wakes up every time she turns over. I know this isn't easy for her, but a couple more weeks and it'll all be over.

Cassius looks up, and it takes one crooked eyebrow for him to climb down off the bed and settle into his bed in the corner of the room.

I follow him over, bending to rub his head.

"You're a good boy, bud. There's even a gift for you under the tree."

He stretches out, and I scratch his belly before standing and walking back to the bed.

Stripping off, I climb under the covers beside Constance and slide my arm underneath her. She sighs then snuggles in as best she can.

"Merry Christmas, sweetness," I whisper, kissing the nape of her neck.

I rest my other hand on her belly, closing my eyes and smiling as the baby shifts. While I know this is our last, I love these moments. Constance's pregnancies have been my greatest joy.

They only make me love my wife even more.

FOUR

OWEN

MY DAUGHTER STANDS in front of me, and my eyes near bug out of my head. "You are *not* going out wearing that." I point to what can only be described as a scarf and little else.

Ava rolls her eyes. "Mum," she calls.

Ginny appears in the doorway. "What's going—" She raises her eyebrows, looking Ava up and down. "Oh, you don't even have to tell me what's going on."

"There's a party at Luke's place, and everyone will be there."

"Except you if you don't go and change into something more suitable," Ginny says.

Ava knits her fingers together. "I got it from your wardrobe. I thought it was fine."

Ginny shifts her gaze to me.

"Ava, Ginny wears a tank top under it. It's not fine for a

sixteen-year-old girl going to a party with sixteen-year-old boys. Who has a party on Christmas Eve anyway?"

Ava shrugs. "Luke's parents said it was okay."

"Do we know Luke's parents?" I ask.

Ginny nods. "They're good people."

I press my lips together. There's nothing to gain by banning her from going. She's not done anything wrong, and whenever I think about how good Ava generally is, I'm reminded about the horror I must have been for my parents.

And I know the minds of sixteen-year-old boys.

I used to be one.

"Fine. But I'm trusting you on this, and I'll pick you up at ten."

Her shoulders slump. "Eleven?"

"Ten. It's Christmas Eve and we've got a big day tomorrow."

"Dad. Please?"

I sigh. "Fine. Ten thirty and not a minute more. But you are wearing something that shows less skin."

"Let me help you find something." Ginny slips her arm around Ava's shoulder and shoots me a wink.

"Thanks." Ava leans her head against Ginny's.

I love my girls. All of them.

But I hate that my daughters have to grow up.

I STARE AT THE WALL, ignoring the television right in front of me.

Ginny dropped Ava at the party an hour ago. She didn't

see Luke's parents, but she's met them through the school and says they're okay. I know a lot of people in Copper Creek, but I don't know everyone. Even so, I'm not sure I trust people who don't shop at my bakery.

Ginny never used to.

Ginny's the exception to my rule.

"Maybe we have to get used to the fact that she's not a little girl anymore." Ginny leans her head on my shoulder.

"I know that. But to me, she's still that little girl who showed up on my doorstep and needed me."

Ginny lifts her head. "Oh, Owen. She'll always need you."

"Sometimes, I'm not so sure about that."

She reaches for my cheek, pulling my face to hers. "Even when she's an adult, off making her own decisions and screwing up her life, you'll always be her father."

"That's just it. I don't want her to screw up her life. Ever."

"That's the only way she's going to learn. It's going to be hard watching her, but if she stumbles, we pick her up."

I smile. "You're so wise. How'd I get lucky enough to find you again?"

"I blame Drew and Hayley. It's their fault for getting married."

Laughing, I wrap my arms around her. "Technically, it's Max's fault for inviting you as his date. And then I stole the girl."

"You can steal me any time, Owen Campbell."

Her smile is luminous. It always is.

But it doesn't quite distract me from the thought that this could still be the longest night of my life.

AT EXACTLY TEN THIRTY, I pull up outside the house.

The blaring music was audible from a street away, but the neighbours are far apart down this rural road, and some of them seem to be having their own celebrations.

I'll give her five minutes.

Someone stumbles out the door. He's obviously drunk as he heads straight for a tree and relieves himself, laughing loudly as he pees.

Shit.

She's not getting five minutes.

I get out of the car and walk toward the front door.

"Mr Campbell."

I turn to see Ava's friend, Kiana, walking toward me. She staggers, and I draw in a deep breath.

"Get in the car."

She stares at me. "But—"

"Do you have anything inside to get?"

She shakes her head.

"Come on."

I steer her toward my car, unlock it, and open the back door. She frowns as she sits in the seat. "I'm going to get Ava. Any idea where she'll be?"

"Shhhhee was with"—she hiccups—"Luke when I s-saw her last." She hiccups again.

"Are Luke's parents here?"

Kiana drops her gaze and shakes her head.

"Stay here. Try not to throw up."

"I'm fine."

"Yeah, right."

I close the door and turn toward the house. I'll drop Kiana off on the way home and let her explain herself to her parents. In the meantime, I need to find my daughter and get her the hell out of here.

Just inside the front door is a couple kissing up a storm. The guy has the girl pressed against the wall, and he's going for a full-on grope with no care about who's watching.

"Break it up, you two."

The girl lets out a long breath like she's relieved when I pull the guy off.

"What do you want?" He eyeballs me.

"I'm looking for Ava Campbell. Or Luke."

He shrugs.

"They were headed upstairs last time I saw them," the blonde girl says.

"Thanks."

She ducks out from beside us and disappears into the living room. I'm going to guess he was being a little aggressive with her, but she's free from him for the moment.

I mount the stairs, my heart beating a little faster with every step. Ava's old enough, legally, to have sex, and I know that, but I'm far from ready for it to be a reality. Not my little girl.

It doesn't take long to find them.

"No. Get off me."

I know that voice anywhere. It comes from behind a closed door to my right.

The door handle jiggles in my hand. I don't like locked doors. Not when my sixteen-year-old is on the other side.

"OPEN THIS DAMN DOOR!" I yell.

"Daddy?"

There's a scream from inside the room, and I move back, ready to shoulder charge the door. I'm not sure if it'll make a difference, but I'll do anything to get to my girl.

With a click, the door opens, and Ava stands on the other side. I expected her to be upset, but instead, she's laughing.

"What's going on?" I take a step into the room.

A teenage boy sits at the base of the bed, cradling his groin.

"We were kissing, but he was on top of me, and I didn't like it."

My eyebrows rise right along with my blood pressure. "Is that why you screamed?"

"I didn't. He did." She leans against me, her laughter filling the room.

"Let's go home." I stare down the boy. "Are you Luke?"

He nods.

"Oh, it's your party? Where are your parents?"

"They went to Carlstown for a party with their friends. They'll be back in a couple of hours."

"Well, I'll be back to talk to them about this, Luke. Let's pack things up and send everyone home." I turn to Ava. "And you and I are going home to talk about why you lied about his parents being here."

Her expression straightens. "I'm sorry, Daddy."

"Those doe eyes aren't going to work on me this time. I put a lot of trust in you, but you betrayed that."

The two of them trail me downstairs until we reach the living room. I turn off the music, and a couple of dozen teenagers turn and look at me.

"Time to go home, kids. Who's been drinking?"

A couple of hands go up. I raise my eyebrows. A few more go up.

"Does anyone need to call parents for a ride? I suggest you do that now. I'll wait."

Deep laughter comes from the corner of the room. I step toward it, to find a presumably drunk smiling boy in the corner. I smirk. "Joe Stephenson's kid. I'm sure I have your dad's number in my phone."

He straightens. "Please don't tell my dad."

"I don't plan to. You're going to call him to come and get you."

He grumbles, but he pulls out his phone.

I turn to look around the room. "That goes for all of you."

It takes a few moments, but, slowly, phones are removed from pockets and the sound of parental conversations fill the room.

Whoever thought me, Owen Campbell, the responsible adult?

I guess wonders will never cease.

WHEN ALL THE kids have been collected by parents, I

turn to Luke. "I'll be back after Christmas. Make sure you tell your mum and dad before I have to."

He nods, shifting his gaze to Ava. "See you later?"

She raises her face and gives him a haughty look I haven't seen since she was little. "Maybe."

This boy's just been kneed in the nuts by her and he's still giving my daughter the heart eyes.

"Come on. We have to drop off Kiana and get home. Your mum will be worried."

Ava looks at her feet. "Sorry, Daddy."

"It's not good enough, Ava. You could have been hurt."

She hangs her head all the way to Kiana's parent's place. Kiana's father is grateful to see her safe and sound, and we soon head home.

"Were you drinking?" I ask. She doesn't smell like alcohol, nor is she unsteady on her feet, but I have to ask.

"No."

I shoot a glance at her as we draw closer to home.

"Dad, I didn't. I swear. The others were, but I knew you'd kill me. You've got too good a sense of smell."

I chuckle. The girls tease me all the time about my talent at sniffing out things. It's the baker in me.

"It's not funny."

"It is if it keeps you from drinking until you're old enough to handle it. Which, at this point in time, is probably going to be about the age of forty-seven."

She crosses her arms and slouches in the seat.

But I'm relieved that she didn't drink. That Luke was ready to take advantage of her when she was sober, rings alarm bells for me. I might be biased because I'm her father, but Ava is the complete package. She's smart, beautiful, and despite my not wanting her to grow up, she's managed to get the Campbell height gene. And maybe because of her past, she's also fiercely independent.

Woe betide any man who thinks they can tell her what to do.

When we reach the house, I turn into the driveway, switch off the car, and get out first, walking around to open the door for Ava.

She flings her arms around my neck. "I'm glad you came to get me."

"I'll always do that. Doesn't matter how old you are." I wrap my arms around my girl and hold her tight. "You can't trust boys. Believe me. I used to be one."

She laughs in my ear.

I pull back a bit. "I love you so much. It'd kill me if anything happened to you."

Tears pool in her eyes, and I feel like the biggest, shitty person despite knowing that I'm not.

"Daddy?" she whispers.

"Yes, Ava?" I wipe her tears with my thumbs. There's one thing I hate and that's seeing any of my girls cry, no matter the circumstances.

"Thank you."

"As if I'd leave you at the party."

"No." She sniffs. "Thank you for always being there for me. I know you don't think I remember, but I'll never forget all the places I stayed before I came to you. You took me in, and you and Mum loved me. And I'll never hurt either of you deliberately."

"I know you wouldn't, sweetheart. And you should know by now that both of us would do anything to keep you safe."

She dips her head.

"You owe your mother an apology too. She had a lot more trust in you than I did."

Ava sighs.

"Let's go inside."

I follow her into the house and just watch her. From the moment I found out I was her dad, I vowed to protect her. And that'll always be the case no matter what. But I'm not sure I'll get through her teenage years in one piece. And I hope like hell she never meets a man like the one I used to be.

I can barely remember a time when she wasn't with me. I sleep-walked through the first thirty years of my life until I found happiness with Ginny, Ava, and then Violet.

I wouldn't give up my girls for anything.

Even the grey hair this one's about to cause me.

Ginny looks up as we walk in the door. "What took you two so long?"

"We ran into some ... difficulties."

"Dad broke the party up and sent everyone home."

Ginny's eyebrows rise. "Really?"

"Luke's parents weren't there. I stepped in. All sorted." I shift my gaze to Ava. "And this one is in trouble." Ginny's brows knit. "She was with Luke who didn't want to take no for an answer."

Ginny's expression crumbles. "Oh, sweetheart. Are you okay?"

Ava drops her gaze. "I'm fine. I don't think Dad is, though."

"I'll be sure to have a word with Luke's parents. If he can't respect our daughter, then he can stay away from her."

"I'm sorry. I'm sorry." She throws her arms around Ginny.

"I know you are, sweetheart. But I need to make sure you understand there are going to be consequences for your actions." I swallow hard. "Tonight's not that night. It's Christmas, and you'll be spending the day with all your cousins tomorrow. I know how much you enjoy that."

She nods.

"Say goodnight to your mother and get to bed."

"Goodnight, Mum."

Ginny gives her a kiss on the head. "Goodnight, Ava. I love you."

"Love you too." With one last small smile, she heads up the hallway toward her bedroom.

I flop down on the couch, pulling Ginny with me.

She laughs, and then I do my best to knock her socks off with a deep kiss.

"For what it's worth, I think you made the right decision to deal with this later."

"I can't be angry with my kid over Christmas." I run my fingers through my hair. "I love her so much, Gin. If anything happened to her ..."

"I know you do."

"Being a parent is so freaking hard. I swear things were much simpler when she was little."

Ginny embraces me. "Probably, but you've always been a good dad. Even when you didn't know what you were doing."

I smile. "I've just been lucky to have you by my side for

all of it. I'm not sure what I would have done if I was completely by myself."

"You were never by yourself."

I turn my head. "You're the best thing that ever happened to me. I hope you know that."

Ginny raises her hand and runs her fingers through my hair. "Feeling's mutual."

For a moment, I'm lost in her eyes. I love this woman so damn much. She came into my life right when I needed her, and I knew from the start I'd never let her go. We went through a lot in those first months. But we came through it together and made our family.

I lean closer and kiss her again, lingering on her lips.

"Ew, gross." Violet walks into the living room. She's the spitting image of Ginny with her red hair.

"There's nothing gross about how much I love your mother." I pull her onto the couch beside me, and she squeals. "I love you just as much. You're supposed to be asleep. How's Santa going to come if you don't go to sleep?"

She rolls her eyes. "Daddy, Santa's not real."

I gape at her. "What? So why do we still leave out milk and cookies?"

"They're for you."

She giggles as I tickle her. "You're too smart. You know that?"

"You and Ava were making so much noise."

I lean my head against hers. "We were, but now it's time for all of us to get some sleep. We're going to see Uncle Adam and Auntie Lily tomorrow."

She pecks me on the cheek. "Love you."

"I love you too. Even when you stop believing in Santa."

"Daddy." She rolls her eyes.

"Want me to tuck you in?"

I already know the answer, but this has become a game. My little miss independent aches to have the freedom her big sister does. But after tonight, I think that freedom will be curtailed for a while.

She nods, which isn't the answer I expect.

"Really?" Ginny asks.

"Santa won't come if I don't go back to sleep." Violet grins, and I laugh out loud.

That's my kid.

FIVE
ADAM

"DAD, CAN WE OPEN OUR PRESENTS?"

Ben stands before me, his hands pressed together like he's praying. Like I haven't given him the answer a hundred times already this morning.

"Just say yes, Dad. It'll shut him up." Rose rolls her eyes and picks at her fingernails.

"Max will be here any minute and then you can go nuts."

Ben crosses his arms and glares. "I don't want to wait."

"We're waiting because he's your brother," I say.

"Just sit down and stop whining, Ben." Rose opens up the recliner and leans back.

I clamp my lips together to stop myself from laughing at my children. Maybe Ben is right, and I should let both him and Rose open their gifts. Lily's a real stickler for tradition, though, and waiting for the whole family to be here before we open the presents is a really big thing for her.

"Hello."

At the sound of Max's voice, Ben's whole face lights up. He might be complaining this morning, and there may be an age gap between them of about fifteen years, but he adores his older brother.

My eldest son steps into the room, and I stand to greet him.

"It's about time you got here," Rose says.

Max carries in a bag of presents and puts them under the tree. "Maybe you can sort these out, squirt."

"I will." Ben rushes toward the bag and grabs it from Max.

"Woah. Slow down, short stuff."

"He's been impatiently waiting for you to arrive." I look back at the door. "Where's Sophie?"

"Mum was outside when we arrived. They're not far away."

"Can we open our presents now?" Ben asks.

Lily walks into the room, Sophie right behind her. "Go for it. We're all here now."

"Morning, Sophie," I say.

She takes a seat on the other side of the room, Max planting himself at her feet. "Good morning."

Lily sits on the couch beside me, leaning on my arm.

Paper's strewn everywhere as Ben rips into his presents, and I take Lily's hand in mine while we watch him.

Since Mum died, Lily's become the matriarch of our whole family. She thrives on it, and Christmas has become her thing to organise. Me? I just love seeing how happy it makes her.

Max stands and holds his hand out to Sophie who takes it with a smile and rises from her seat.

"Mum, Dad, there's something Sophie and I want to tell you."

I tilt my head. "What is it?"

"I asked Sophie to marry me, and she said yes."

My mouth falls open. "That's fantastic." I reach for Lily's hand.

She's smiling up at Max with tears welling in her eyes. "Oh, Max. I'm so happy for you," she says.

"There's something else too," Sophie says, exchanging a glance with Max.

Max nods. "We're having a baby."

All the colour drains from Lily's face. "You're having a baby?" she whispers.

I squeeze Lily's hand tight and smile. "Are you okay?"

For a moment, she just gazes at Max. She drops her gaze and nods. "It's a little overwhelming."

Max's lips twitch. "Mum, it's okay. You're still young to be a grandmother."

Turning back to Lily, I cock my head. "Is that what's up with you? You don't like the idea of becoming a granny?"

Lily's eyes widen. "Oh my God! No. It's not that."

"What's wrong?"

She shakes away my hand and stands, walking to the other side of the room to get the family album. All of a sudden it hits me, but I wait for her to return so she can tell us.

"When you were born," she says, sitting and opening the

album to a well-worn page. "I didn't even know if you would live or die. You were so small, and they told me you'd never be likely to have a normal life." She points at the photo of the tiny baby in the incubator. "But you fought, and you won, Max. And now you're going to be a father and I couldn't be prouder of you."

"Mum." Max drops to his knees in front of her. "I thought you were upset."

Lily shakes her head, raising her palm to his cheek. "No, sweetheart. I love you so much, and I'm so happy that you found Sophie. And now the two of you are getting married and having a baby." She places the album on the arm of the couch and stands. "I guess we have a wedding coming up and a baby to prepare for."

"We thought a January wedding—the baby's due in May," Sophie says.

"I'm so happy for you both." Lily embraces Sophie, and I have to admit it even makes me tear up a little.

The odds were against Max. When I came back into his life, I couldn't have predicted the man who now stands in front of me. He struggled for so long with his learning disability until Ginny became his schoolteacher and took him under her wing. Finishing his education helped give him confidence, and he's now a hell of a mechanic.

I push myself off the couch and walk over to him. My pride in Max is overwhelming, and we don't exchange any words before he ends up in my arms. I hug him tight.

"Dad?" Max asks.

"Yes, son?"

"Will you be my best man?"

I let him go but nod and grip his arms. "I'd be honoured."

Dropping my hands, I lean over and kiss Sophie on the cheek. "Anything you two need, just let us know."

Sophie beams. "Of course."

I know Sophie has her mother—it was just the two of them for a few years, but they're both a part of our family now. Her mother would be with us today, but she's gone away to spend Christmas with friends. When she comes back, I'm sure she'll be planning everything with Lily and Sophie.

I can't believe my boy's getting married.

"I'm going to make a coffee. Who wants one?" Lily asks.

Once she has the numbers, she turns and heads toward the kitchen.

"Is she really okay?" Sophie asks.

I pause for a moment. "Lily loves the two of you so much. I'm sure this'll be overwhelming in some ways, but you know she'll be with you every step of the way."

Sophie smiles. "I haven't told my mum yet. We wanted you to be the first to know."

Max slips his arm around her. "Sophie's mum's back the day after tomorrow and we'll tell her then. I wanted this to be a Christmas present."

"And it's the best gift that you could have given us. We're so proud of you. Both of you." I draw a deep breath. "I'll go check on Lily. Today's going to be emotional for her. Excuse me."

I walk out of the living room and toward the kitchen where my wife stands at the bench, tapping her fingernails on the stainless-steel sink surround.

For a moment, I watch her as the kettle flicks off, and she pours the hot water into the mugs.

"Lily, are you okay?"

She turns to look at me. "Yes. Why wouldn't I be?"

"That's some pretty big news Max dropped on us." I make my way over to her and pull her into my arms. "I know how hard it was for you when he first moved out."

She blows out a long breath. "That was tough. But he's been with Sophie for a long time now, and this is a natural progression. He couldn't have picked a better partner. She's so good for him."

"And the rest?"

"We're going to be grandparents, Adam." Her blue eyes shine with happiness.

"Congratulations, Grandma." I press a kiss to her forehead. "Should we join the others?"

She slaps me on the chest. "Not so much of the grandma stuff."

"I thought it wouldn't bother you."

"Max and Sophie having a baby doesn't bother me. You calling me Grandma, does."

I grin. "Wait until Corey gets hold of this news."

Lilly pauses before rolling her eyes. "Oh God. You're right."

"Not to mention Drew."

She sucks on her lower lip. "Can we just not go to Christmas dinner?"

"I'm not sure you can get out of it given that we're hosting."

Lily laughs. "I guess we have to face them all at some point."

I lean in and nuzzle her neck. "Sexiest grandmother ever."

"You're not so bad for a grandad yourself."

"Might have to give you an early Christmas present tonight."

She sighs when I reach her collarbone. "What would that be?"

"Me, you, our bed."

"That sounds wonderful to me."

SIX

COREY

I LOVE CHRISTMAS MORNING.

The kids are always up early to check out what's under the tree, and any other day of the year I'd be grumpy, but the joy in their voices when they storm into our bedroom to beg us to get out of bed makes me smile.

"Dad, come on." Isla tugs on my hand.

I pry an eye open and mumble, "What? Why?"

"Santa's been, Dad."

I open my eyes and smile at her. "Really? I thought Christmas was tomorrow. Is he early?"

She rolls her eyes. "Daaaad."

"Can we open our presents?" Oscar asks.

I reach over and tap him on the nose. "You know the rules. We'll have to see if Mum's awake yet."

Eli's taking care of that. Constance opens one eye at his gentle prodding. "What time is it?"

"Just after six thirty."

"Can't we sleep another hour?" she groans.

I laugh. "Maybe in a few more years." Leaning over, I kiss her hair. "I'll make you breakfast in bed tomorrow, at a much more acceptable hour."

"That sounds fair." She scans the room. "We'll be out in a minute. Just go and wait in the living room."

Constance's tired grey eyes tell a story of their own.

"If you want to stay in bed and sleep, the kids can wait to open their presents."

She shakes her head. "No. I'll be fine. Just give me a minute to get out of bed."

"Are you okay?"

"Just a bit crampy. And I wish I could roll over without having to negotiate my every move." She lets out a strained laugh.

"I'll just grab some pants and help you."

I slide out of bed and open a drawer, pulling out a clean pair of trackpants. Constance sighs as I tug them on.

"What?" I ask.

"I just love the way you look in those. Always did. The way they sit on your hips." She lets out a low whistle.

I grin and walk around the bed. "As long as it makes you happy."

"You make me happy." She pushes herself up into a seated position and takes my hand.

"Are you ready?" I ask.

Constance nods. "It's not that far to the couch. I'll be fine."

"I'll make you breakfast. That might help."

"You're so good to me." She drops her feet to the floor, and I help her up.

"I just love taking care of my lady." I place my hand on her belly. "You do such an amazing job of looking after all of us, and I hope you know how much I love you."

Her eyes are so full of emotion. "I've never doubted your love for me, Corey. Not for a second. Even when I'm all bloaty."

"You're always beautiful to me." I bend and give her a tender kiss, lingering on her lips.

"MUM! DAD!" Eli yells.

I chuckle. "I think we're wanted."

"They can wait another minute while I kiss my husband."

I lean in again. "I like the way you think."

———

FROM THE KITCHEN, I watch Constance. She's in her element. Almost all the presents have been opened, and our children are pre-occupied with their toys. Every so often, they stop to show her something, and she beams at them, taking interest in the gifts she wrapped as if she's never seen them before.

"Here you go." I carry in the coffee she asked for, and the plate of hot buttered toast.

"Thank you." She smiles as I place them on the table in front of her.

"Hey, guys, can you find Mum's present under the tree? The one from me?"

I sit beside her on the couch, right as she winces.

"Are you up to today? We could give it a miss. Everyone would understand."

She smiles. "I'll be fine. I'm just sore. You might just have to feed me Christmas lunch."

I pick up her coffee mug from the table and lift it to her lips. "I'd be more than happy to. But we can stay home."

She swallows a mouthful of her drink and takes her cup from me, placing it back on the table as she runs her tongue over her lips.

"The kids are so looking forward to it. We don't have to stay all day," she pleads.

Reluctantly, I nod. "On one condition. That you tell me the instant you need out of there. You can't fool me. I can see how tired you are."

She reaches for my hand and squeezes it. "I know I can't get anything past you."

I dip my head to kiss her knuckles. "We'll go, let the kids open their presents, have lunch, and then come home."

"That sounds good."

"And I'm going to be watching the whole time. I'll throw you over my shoulder and carry you home if I have to."

She laughs. "Remember when we first met? I was so angry when you did that."

"I'd do it again in a heartbeat."

"This one says, 'To Constance from Corey.' Is that it?" Isla asks.

"That's the one."

She carries it to her mother and pauses long enough for me to grab her around the waist and pull her down on my lap.

My daughter giggles and slides her arms around my neck.

"I thought we decided that we were only getting presents for the kids." Tears well in her eyes as she looks at the gold foil wrapping.

"You know me. I've never been good at following rules."

Constance leans over and kisses me softly. "I guess I'd better see what it is." She tugs on the ribbon, and it falls open. Inside the wrapping is a navy-blue velvet box.

"Corey," she growls.

"Just open it."

Her lips curl into a smile as she unfolds the box.

It's a ring. Similar to her engagement ring, it's a gold band with diamonds embedded it in.

"What's this?"

I smile. "An eternity ring, to go with that engagement and wedding ring of yours. I should have done it a long time ago." I cock my head. "But, soon, our family will be complete, and it seemed like a good time to do it."

"Oh, Corey." Her mouth falls open, and a tear escapes and rolls down her left cheek. "You shouldn't have."

"Of course I should. You deserve it. You're the core of our family, Con, and I couldn't have achieved what I have these past ten years without you."

Tears escape and roll down her cheeks.

"I'm not sure it'll fit until after the baby's born."

I chuckle, releasing Isla and pulling Constance into my arms. "Not long to go now, then."

She snuggles in against me. "Thank you," she whispers.

"I love you, sweetness."

"I love you too. How much was it?"

I plant a kiss on her temple. "I've been saving a little every week since the start of the year for it."

"Your beer money." She laughs.

"And you didn't even notice I've barely had any." I squeeze her shoulders. "You're worth it."

"Well, I have been a bit busy with this." She runs her hand across her baby bump and grimaces.

"Are you sure you're okay?"

"I'll be fine. I think I just need to get up and move a bit. Let the kids open the rest of their presents and we'll get going. There's a pavlova in the fridge to take, and the presents for the rest of the family are—"

"I've got it." I grin. "I'll throw your bag in the back as well, now I'm on holiday."

Even with a home birth planned, Constance has a bag of baby things packed in case we need to go anywhere.

"Good idea. I'm going to get dressed. Be back in a minute."

My eyes don't leave her as she pushes herself off the couch and walks to the bedroom. She's clearly putting up a front, but how uncomfortable is she?

All I know is that I'll be keeping a close watch on her today.

IT'S a little after ten when we reach an already packed Lily's and Adam's place. They have the biggest house out of everyone. Until we finish building our new home. So it makes sense that when we get together for Christmas, it's their place we gather at.

Eli, Isla, and Oscar scatter to play with their cousins, and I open up the back of the SUV. Cassius jumps out. He loves coming here. Adam and Lily have a large backyard, and the kids will play with him without giving him a hard time.

Constance smiles as I open her door and offer her my arm. "Thank you."

"It's what I'm here for."

She gets to her feet outside the car and takes a breath. "I'll take the pavlova in. You grab the presents."

"I can take it all."

"I'm not completely useless, Corey," she grumps at me, and I cock an eyebrow.

"You're far from useless. But I thought as your doting husband, I'd take you inside where you can put your feet up, and then I can do all the labour."

She glares at me.

"Okay. Bad choice of words." I laugh. "Come on. Forget the pavlova. I'll come back in a minute and grab everything."

I don't worry any less as I help her up the steps and into the house.

Lily swoops in the second we walk through the door. "Constance, how are you? I saved you a spot." She points toward the couch, and Constance makes her way to it.

Lily looks at me. "Is she okay?"

I nod. "Just over being pregnant, I think."

"I know how that feels."

"I'll just pop back to the car and grab the rest of our

things and be back in a minute. Can you please keep an eye on her?"

Lily laughs. "What are you worried about? She's in the best place to be taken care of. Drew and Hayley are already here."

I cast my gaze around the room until I meet Drew's eyes. He nods, raising his coffee cup, and I nod back in response. His gaze shifts, and I follow it, smiling when I realise it rests on Constance.

Eli runs up to me. "Dad, do you want me to help bring in the presents?"

"Sure, bud. Let's go get them now."

I look back over at Constance. Drew's with her now, squatting in front of her. She laughs, and I know he's got this. It doesn't make me worry any less.

Turning, I head back out to the car and open the boot. Constance packed the gifts in two boxes, and I grab the lighter one of the two and hand it to Eli.

"Put these under the tree and I'll be there in a minute with the other lot."

He nods, beaming as he carries off the gifts. For a moment, I watch him. I'm so proud of my son.

I pick up the box and close the boot before picking up the pavlova from its safe place on the floor under the passenger seat.

"I'll take that." Lily grabs it from me right as I walk in the door.

"That's my pavlova, you know." I call after her. "Constance made it for *me*."

Unsure if that tactic will work, I walk back into the

living room and deposit the box on the floor near the tree. Eli's already unpacked the first one, and he grabs the second. For a moment, I just watch him, and content he's got things under control, I turn to greet the rest of the family.

It takes a while because there are so damn many now.

I love seeing Max and Sophie here. I'll always think of Max as that awkward kid who questioned everything and never held back. To see him as a grown man with a partner and a career gives me a lot of pride.

It's also hard to reconcile little Ava with the young woman who's hanging out with her younger cousins with no complaints. The younger ones look up to her, and she never gets impatient with them.

"Princess." I approach Hayley and she beams. Drew hates it when I call her that. It's his pet name for her, and while I don't use it as a general rule, it's always a good start to winding him up.

"Hey." She smiles as I plant a kiss on her cheek.

"How was your trip?"

Hayley runs her finger around the rim of her glass. "Pretty uneventful. I think Drew's having a mid-life crisis, but we made it."

"Oh?"

"He's not really handling the kids getting older very well. But it's not like we can do anything about that." She shrugs.

"No. Once they're out, there's no reversing that process."

"And now you're about to go through it all again."

I nod. "For the last time."

She places her hand on my arm. "I remember when Alex

was born, and Drew and I decided we weren't going to have any more. It's a weird feeling."

I draw in a deep breath. "Constance has struggled a lot more this time. I'm glad we made the decision."

Shifting my gaze across the room, I lay eyes on my wife again. She's leaning back on the couch and her eyes are closed. I'd give anything to take that tiredness away from her so that she didn't have to go through it.

"I'm going to check up on Con. Talk to you later."

Hayley squeezes my arm. "Sure thing."

I walk across the room. It's filled with chatter and laughter from both the kids and the adults, but there's only one person I'm concerned with right now.

As I draw close, Constance sucks in a breath.

"Constance?"

I don't need to say anything else. When she raises her gaze to me, I see a look I haven't seen in a while. "Drew. I think we need some help here."

My brother walks over to us. "What's up?"

"I think the baby's on its way." Constance says as if this happens every day of our life. A small smile lights her eyes as she exhales, slowly.

Drew sits on the couch beside her. "Tell me what's going on."

In an instant, he switches from relaxed brother to doctor.

"I thought they were Braxton Hicks. And I talked to my midwife last night"—Constance grimaces again, letting out short puffy breaths—"I was talking to you half an hour ago, and I felt okay. Not anymore."

Drew pats her knee and turns his head. "Lily, Hayley.

Could you please come over here?" He turns back to Constance, a smile on his face. "It'll be okay. You've got the dream team here."

"Is everything okay?" Hayley rests her hand on Drew's shoulder.

"Can you grab Lily and prepare their spare room for Constance to give birth?"

Her eyes widen and she winks. "Sure. No time like the present."

She disappears, and for a moment I feel helpless. I've never been gladder to have Drew and Hayley with us. The midwife isn't that far away, but I'm not sure given our past deliveries that she'd get here in time.

There's a sharp intake of breath from Constance, and Drew checks his watch. "Yeah, that's a good sign. Once we get into that room, we'll examine you and see how close we are." He looks up at me. "Looks like you two are having a Christmas baby."

"I'm so sorry," Constance says.

"Babies don't stick to timetables. You'll be fine," Hayley says softly.

I reach for her hand. "I'm right here. I knew something was up."

Her eyes grow wide and she playfully whacks my arm. "You could have told *me*."

I laugh.

"Now's not the time, Corey." Drew narrows his eyes at me.

I know these things can get a little out of control. Oscar's birth was faster than Eli's by a long shot. Isla almost crawled out, it happened so quickly.

I run my thumb across the back of Con's hand. "I'm sorry. I just want you to be okay."

"It's alright. I thought we'd get through today without any drama."

"Have you met our family?" I grin.

"I guess I should be used to it by now." Constance laughs then grimaces.

"Drew. The bed's sorted," Hayley calls.

Constance pushes herself up, but there's no way I'm letting her move another step.

I scoop her into my arms. I'm not sure she even realises the back of her dress is soaked, but nothing else matters other than getting her into that room and having this baby safely delivered.

"Corey, I'm sorry."

"What for?"

"Ruining a family day."

I chuckle. "You're not ruining anything. It's not like you can keep the baby in. You're about to become a mother again, sweetness."

"With the best father on the planet." She leans her head against my shoulder as I carry her up the hallway.

"Just in here," Lily squeezes my shoulder. "Good luck."

Hayley smiles at us as we enter the room. The bed's been stripped back but has plenty of sheets and towels down. Constance has never given birth anywhere other than our house, and I know this'll make her nervous.

"How are you doing, Constance?" Hayley asks.

Con nods. "I'm okay. Just really ready to get this over with."

Hayley smiles. "I know. Lily left a couple of nightgowns if you want to get this dress off."

Constance nods again.

I help her to her feet and carefully lift her dress up and over her head. Hayley takes a towel and dries down the back of her legs while I get the nightgown on her and her panties off. The gown is soft and dry, and Constance gives me a weak smile when we're done.

"Thank you."

"You're only gonna get the best of care." I stroke her cheek before helping her onto the bed.

She lets out a long breath of relief as she lies down. "I know. I managed to time this right. Or someone did." She pats her stomach before screwing up her face again. "Oww. That one hurt."

"I'll take a look and we'll see how it's going." Hayley smiles. "Corey, do you want to give the midwife a call and let her know the situation?"

"Sure. I'll let her know Con's in good hands."

Hayley pushes up the nightgown, and Constance parts her legs. It only takes a moment. "You're already at nine centimetres. Just need to get you to ten. Won't be long before your baby's here." She smiles, and it's reassuring. "Drew's just gone to get his bag from the car."

I guess that's what makes her and Drew such a good team. I've seen his bedside manner, and it's just as good.

"I'll make that call. Be back in a minute."

"Don't take too long." Hayley flashes me a reassuring smile.

I step out of the room and find a quiet spot where I can make a call. Ava's got my kids under control by the looks of things—they don't even seem to have noticed their mother's no longer in the room.

The phone rings twice before she answers.

"Hey, Christine. It's Corey Campbell."

"Corey? What can I do for you?"

"Con's in labour. Her water's broken. Hayley and Drew are here, and they've got a bed set up. Hayley says Constance is at nine centimetres and to call you. We're at Adam's house."

"She's progressed fast. I'm about half an hour away, so I'll grab my things and come over. Sounds like Hayley's got it under control."

I blow out a breath. "Yeah. I'm relieved we're here to be honest with the way things have gone. We'll be glad to see you. Sorry to call you on Christmas Day."

She laughs. "Babies can be impatient, and let's face it, Constance is in the right place."

"I'm gonna apologise in advance if Drew gets a little pushy. You know what doctors are like."

"I sure do. As long as Constance gets the care she needs, I'm sure we can all work together."

"I'm sure you can. See you soon."

After I've hung up the call, I look at the phone. "Good luck with that," I mutter.

I know Drew. And I know that when he met Hayley, she was taking care of Lily while she delivered Rose. I remember her saying Drew got under her feet, and somehow also managed to worm his way into her heart.

He's going to be a real pain in the arse for Christine.

Turning, I walk back into the living room. It's full of noise as the kids all chat as if they haven't been reunited in months. The reality is, with the exception of Drew's children, all the Campbell offspring spend a lot of time together, and with the long stretch of summer holiday ahead of them, they'll see each other nearly every day.

"Eli," I call.

His head shoots up. "Yeah, Dad?"

"Can you grab your brother and sister and come over here?"

His brows knit, and he looks toward the couch where his mother had been sitting. He leans over and grabs Isla's hand, and I'm not sure what he says to Oscar, but the three of them run over to me.

"Where's Mum?" Eli asks.

I squat in front of them to lower myself for Isla. "That's what I wanted to talk to you three for. Mum's having the baby."

Isla's eyes grow wide, and Oscar slides his hand into mine.

"She'll be okay. Uncle Drew and Auntie Hayley are in there with her, and they help mums have their babies all the time. I'm going to go and sit with her, so I wanted you three to know you're getting your brother or sister for Christmas."

Isla claps. "The baby's coming, Daddy."

I stroke her hair with my free hand. "Yes, they are, little sweetness. Can you stay with Ava until I come back in here?"

Oscar wraps his arms around my neck, and I give him a squeeze.

"I'll take care of them," Eli says.

I straighten up and grip his shoulder. "I know you will. I'll be back out when I have some news."

Isla and Oscar are already gone—returned to the corner where Ava's sitting.

"Corey," Lily says as she approaches. "We'll hold off the present opening for a while. I've got some snacks the kids can have. It's still pretty early in the day."

"Sounds great. Thanks for everything."

She shifts her gaze to the kids. "You're welcome. It's just making the day extra special. I'll take care of them."

"Appreciate it."

Taking a deep breath, I make my way back to the bedroom and Constance. She's my whole world, and while I trust her midwife, I'm so glad Drew and Hayley are here too.

"She's on her way, sweetness." I sit on the side of the bed and Constance takes hold of my hand. She lets out a loud moan, gripping me tightly.

"I hope she's not long. This baby's not going to wait for her," Drew says.

"That close?"

He focuses his gaze on me. "Contractions are coming thick and fast now. I'm just glad you're back so Constance can destroy the skin on your hands."

Con stares at him. "Did I hurt you?"

"I'm fine. Just make sure you hold his hand from now on. He's got tougher skin than I do." Drew chuckles.

Her pained expression makes me steel myself for what's

about to come, and sure enough she digs her nails into me. "Oooh."

"I think it's time to check you again." Hayley moves into place. "Are you okay with me taking another look, Constance?"

Con nods. "Please."

Hayley seems to exhale a long breath as she examines her. "Oh, this little one is so ready. Next contraction you can start pushing."

It all seems to go so quickly after that. Isla's birth was so fast, and this little one seems as determined to arrive. I'm not even sure how many times she pushes, but each one takes us closer to meeting our baby.

"We can do this," I say in hope of encouraging her.

Constance's eyes blaze in anger. "We?"

"I'm sorry?"

She fixes her gaze on me, sweat beading on her brow. "This is the fourth time *I've* done this, Corey."

I flinch, and Drew snickers. "Sorry, sweetness. You're a machine."

"Never letting you near me again." She grunts, her face distorting.

"Come on, Con. You can do it." Drew's words of encouragement seem to steel Constance's resolve and she grits her teeth.

I could kiss Drew for the way him and Hayley have taken care of my girl.

Constance grips my hand.

"One more. Let's see what we've got this time."

She nods, and as the pain overtakes her, her nails dig into my skin.

With some ear-piercing screams, pain shooting up my arm, and undeniable strength from my wife, it's over.

"Constance, she's beautiful," Hayley says.

"She? We've got another girl?" Tears run down Con's face, but my heart's so full. Seeing her so happy after she's been in so much pain is like the sun coming out from behind a cloud.

"You do. A very healthy, very alert baby girl." Drew grins. "Congratulations, you two."

The door opens and Christine walks in. She smiles a broad smile at all of us. "Did I just miss it?"

"By maybe a minute?" I say.

"Let me have a look." She stands behind Hayley. "Oh, she's beautiful."

"We'll just check her over and then you can have a cuddle," Hayley says.

Drew holds out a pair of scissors. "Did you want to cut the cord, Corey?"

My heart thuds. This is one of those moments that etches itself in your brain forever. I have so much admiration for Constance giving birth four times, but this is the part I play. It was me who cut the older children's cords, and this one will be no different.

I take them from him. "You know I do."

He hands me the scissors and holds the cord up so I can make the cut.

"Where's Lily with those towels?" Hayley asks.

"Here." Lily arrives with a pile of towels she's been

warming and places them on the end of the bed. "I'll get out of your way and be back in a little bit to visit."

"How about you lie down with your mama?" Hayley places our girl on Con's chest. She takes the towels and places a couple on top of the baby.

"Hi," I say, stroking the baby's head with my index finger. "You are so much like your mother." And just like I did with our other three children, I fall madly in love with my newest daughter the moment I set eyes on her.

Just as I fell for their mother.

"Do you really think so?" Constance says.

"Her eyes are grey."

"All babies are like that."

"The others had blue eyes. Not this one."

I study my daughter closely. "Hey, little sweetness."

"You can't call her little sweetness. That's Isla's."

I frown. "What can I call her, then?"

Constance shrugs. "You'll work it out."

Leaning over, I give my wife a soft kiss on the lips. I'm so grateful for this woman every single day, and especially in this moment.

Our family is complete.

"CAN WE COME IN?"

I'm not even sure how much time has passed when I hear Lily's voice. Around us, Hayley and Christine have cleaned up, and Drew has managed to stay out of their way as our little one has her first feed.

"Please," Constance calls out.

Lily's got such a wistful look on her face as she walks back into the room. She and Constance are really close, and I think she's been looking forward to this moment almost as much as we have.

"Here she is." Constance rocks the baby.

Lily draws closer. "Oh, she's so beautiful." She sits on the end of the bed. "Stay the night. You look so comfortable, and it's easy to find space for the kids. Let us take care of them," Lily says.

"Are you sure?" Constance asks.

"Adam's just gone to get the portacot out of storage. It's not perfect, but it'll work for tonight if you want to use it. Rest up and enjoy your new baby."

"Thank you." Constance leans against me.

"It's my pleasure. I'll be happy to take her for cuddles later. You won't be short on volunteers for that." Lily grins. "It's nice to have a baby in the house again. Even if it's just for the night."

"I really appreciate all of this, Lil," I say.

She grips my arm. "You two have had a crazy day. We'll all take good care of both of you."

Adam walks in with the portable cot in one hand and the mattress in the other. "Not sure if you want to use this, but I thought it might be useful."

"Thank you," I say. "Have the kids had their presents yet?"

Lily shakes her head. "We wanted to wait until everyone was together."

I look over at Drew. "Are we good to move Constance?"

He rolls his eyes at me. "This is your fourth baby. Don't you know the routine by now?"

"Sure, but we're out of our element here. If we were home, I'd just move everything into the bedroom so Constance didn't have to go anywhere."

Con kisses my cheek. "I'll be fine. Can you go and grab my baby bag from the car? Then I can have a shower and join you all. Are you okay with her for a little while?"

"I'll take her out to meet her siblings."

Constance squeezes my arm. "Good idea. I'll be out soon."

"There's no hurry. The kids can wait."

"I'll make sure there's a spot on the couch for you," Lily says. "It's the most comfortable place to sit in the living room."

"Dude. Dad just arrived. We'll get him settled in, and when Constance is ready, we'll start opening presents. Max has an announcement too," Adam says from the doorway

I grin. "That's great. I can't wait for Dad to meet her."

"What are you going to call her?"

I meet Constance's gaze. "Well, we thought we might name her Joanna, after Mum."

Adam's smile widens. "Dad'll like that."

"I thought it was about time. I'm only sorry she didn't get to meet any of my kids."

Adam gives me a short, sharp nod. His feelings about that are bound to be complex given Mum's indifference to Max. It took a long time for any reconciliation to happen after he came back to town, and then there was only a short time before Mum died.

She missed out on so much, but there was so much she chose to miss out on.

"I'll head out there and leave you to it. See you in the living room?"

Constance drops her hand. "I won't be too long."

"Take your time. The kids can wait a bit longer."

I carry my tiny bundle into the living room. All the children are gathered around the tree, waiting for the moment when they can get stuck in.

"Eli, Oscar, Isla, come and meet you little sister."

The three of them run over as I sit on the couch.

Isla's eyes are so wide. "She's so small."

"So were you once."

She softly bops the baby on the nose. "Hello, baby sweetness."

I chuckle. In one move, Isla's solved my dilemma.

Baby sweetness indeed.

SEVEN

MAX

I TAKE a deep breath and wait for Constance to take a seat. I'm really glad she could join us—giving birth on Christmas day in Mum and Dad's house must be a bit crazy for her.

And now I have a new little cousin.

"What's going on?" Owen asks.

I grin. "Well ... I asked Sophie to marry me, and she said yes."

All I see are beaming faces.

"Dude! That's fantastic. Congratulations," Corey says.

I take a deep breath. "There's more. We're having a baby."

At that, my aunts and uncles cheer, and my grandfather gets to his feet. He's spritely for a man in his 70s, and these past ten years, we've grown close.

"Max, that's wonderful. I'm going to be a great-grandfather."

"You sure are, Poppa."

He walks toward me and gives me a big hug. "I'm so proud of you. And Sophie. I'm so happy for both of you."

She closes her eyes as he hugs her. Sophie's got one grandparent, just like I do, but he lives on the South Island. Poppa just adopted her as one of his own without question. Sometimes I think he's trying to make up for the years he wasn't in my life, but none of that matters now.

"Thank you," Sophie says.

Poppa reaches for my arm. "I missed so much of you when you were little, Max. I want you to know I'll be there for your child."

I swallow hard. For years I had nothing to do with my grandparents, but every so often some mysterious benefactor would drop off boxes of clothing and supplies to the little house Mum and I lived in. It wasn't until Dad came back that we found out it was Poppa.

He always supported me even when my grandmother didn't want anything to do with us.

I grip his hand. "I know."

He turns to go back to his seat, and I let out a long breath.

"Hey, kiddo." Corey walks over to us. Sophie's eyes light up at the sight of the baby, and I don't miss the little sigh she lets out. Neither does Corey from the way his lips curl into a smile. "Want to hold her?"

Sophie gasps. "I'd love to."

He gently lifts the baby into her arms, and my heart swells at the sight. He's such a big guy, physically, and the baby's tiny in his hands, but she fills Sophie's arm quite nicely.

I've got a lump in my throat so big that it's hard to swallow.

"Look at her, Max. She's so precious."

"That'll be you two soon enough with your own," Corey says. "How did your mum take the news she'll be a grandma?"

I laugh. "She's a bit overwhelmed by the news."

"I bet." Corey grips my shoulder. "I'm so proud of you."

"Thanks."

"I mean it, Max. Look at you. From that goofy kid to this responsible adult with a kid on the way. I couldn't be more proud." He drops his hand. "I had an idea a while ago, but now it seems more relevant to you."

"What is it?"

"Our new house is nearly done. Some of the utilities still need to be finished off, but once that's done, we'll be moving in, and I'm sure I've told you my plans are to get the old house moved onto the section I bought closer to town."

I nod. Corey's been planning this move for several years. And now the baby's here, they'll be needing the extra space.

"My plan was to get that done and finish it off so we could rent it out. I've been thinking for a while that it'd be good for you two, but with this baby coming, you'll need more space than the flat you're in."

Smiling, I glance at Sophie. We've been living in Owen's old flat behind the bakery for the past two years. Corey's right. There's enough room for the three of us. But having more space would be good.

"I'd be keen."

"We'll talk soon, but it seems logical to me."

"What seems logical?" Mum approaches with Dad by her side.

"Max and I are talking houses. We're going to work together to find him some more space," Corey says.

Mum smiles. "That's wonderful."

"Anyway, look at you, hottest grandma in Copper Creek." Corey grins.

Dad waves his index finger at Corey. "Don't you start anything ..."

"Relax. I'm really happy for you two. And if you'll excuse me, I think I'd better get this one back to her mother." He holds his arms out, and Sophie returns the baby with a contented sigh.

He turns and carries her back to the couch.

Sophie slides her hand into mine. "She's so cute. Another few months and that will be us."

I place a kiss in her hair. "Can't wait."

"Do you really think we could move into Corey's old house?"

I squeeze her hand. "Would you want to?"

That hopeful look in her eyes tells me what she's thinking before she says it. "It's a lovely house. And Corey would make sure it was ready for us." Her smile radiates the room. "It's a real home, Max. I mean, the flat is nice, but ..."

"I agree."

For a moment, I'm lost in her eyes. There's still a part of me that can't quite believe I have Sophie in my life. I had the biggest crush on her in high school, and it wasn't until after we left that I came to realise she felt the same way.

"That's settled, then."

Mum turns and claps her hands to get everyone's attention. "This has been a crazy day so far, and it's not even lunch time. Why don't we hand out the presents so at least the kids can have something to play with," Mum says.

"Good thinking." Dad plants a kiss on her neck and makes his way to the tree. Sophie follows behind him, leaving Mum and me.

"I really am so proud of you." Mum looks at me with so much love, just as she always has. For as long as I can remember, it's been the one constant in my life. Even when it was just the two of us, and things were really rough for her, my relationship with her never wavered.

"You told me this already." I smile.

She laughs. "I know, but I love you so much and I'll always be proud. And now you get to marry your first love and start your own family. I'm so happy, Max."

I wrap my arms around her, and she buries her face in my chest.

"There's no way I could have done any of this without you, Mum. If I'm half as good at this parenting thing than you, I'll be one of the best."

There are tears in her eyes when she raises her head. "I think I did okay."

"You did better than okay. I'm awesome."

Mum laughs again, letting me go to wipe her tears away. "Don't you ever change."

"I'm pretty sure it's too late for that."

She runs her gaze over my face. "I'm not sure how Sophie puts up with you."

I shrug. "You put up with me for a lot longer."

"And I don't regret a single moment."

"I'm sure that's not true."

Mum lifts her hand to my face and cups my cheek. "I love you, Max."

"Love you too, Mum."

"Want to go and open your presents?"

I peck her on the cheek. I love Christmas so much and she knows it. "You bet."

And as I head toward the tree, I think about all the Christmas days when it was just Mum and me. It was a long time ago, but it's always meant I don't take what I have now for granted.

And I never will.

Coming soon Solid Ground

Stand alones

For the Love of Chloe

Only Ever You

The Friends Duet

Loving Rowan

Three Days

The Forever Series

Something Real

The Right One

Unexpected

Chances Series

Another Chance

Taking Chances

Lifetime Series

In a Lifetime

In an Instant

In a Heartbeat

In the End

At the Start

ABOUT THE AUTHOR

Wendy Smith is a multi-platform bestselling author, whose book In the End, written as Ariadne Wayne, was named one of Apple's best books of 2017. She lives with her two children and two cats in New Zealand where she bases her books because she loves living there. All her stories come with a quirky sense of humour, and she cries over everything.

Find me online
www.wendysmith.co.nz
wendy@wendysmith.co.nz

f X ⓞ

Milton Keynes UK
Ingram Content Group UK Ltd.
UKHW031213111124
451035UK00007B/750

9 781991 303080